MEG and MOG

for Loveday

MEG and MOG

by Helen Nicoll
and Jan Pieńkowski

PUFFIN BOOKS

Once upon a time
there was a witch
called Meg

At midnight
the owl hooted 3 times
and woke her up

She got out of bed
to dress for
the spell party

her long
black cloak

and her tall
black hat

In the kitchen
lay her big
striped cat Mog
He was
fast asleep

She trod on Mog's tail

At 1 o'clock she got her broomstick her cauldron and a spider

and
she
flew
up
the
chimney
with
Mog

Up in the sky

she met her friends
going to the party
Bess
Jess
Tess
and Cress

They landed on a hill
in the moonlight
to make the spell

Each of them
had brought something
to put in the cauldron

This is what
they put in:

a
beetle

a frog

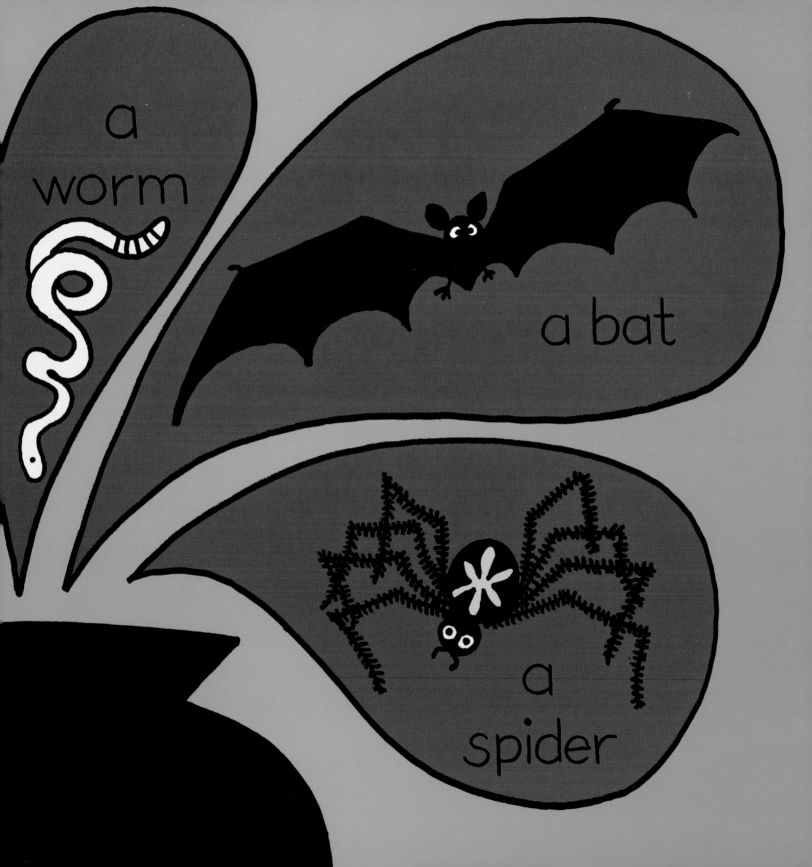

ABRACAD

They all
stirred the cauldron
as they chanted
their spell

There was
a flash
and a bang

OM

Something had gone wrong

Bess, Jess,
Tess and Cress
all changed into mice
and Mog chased them

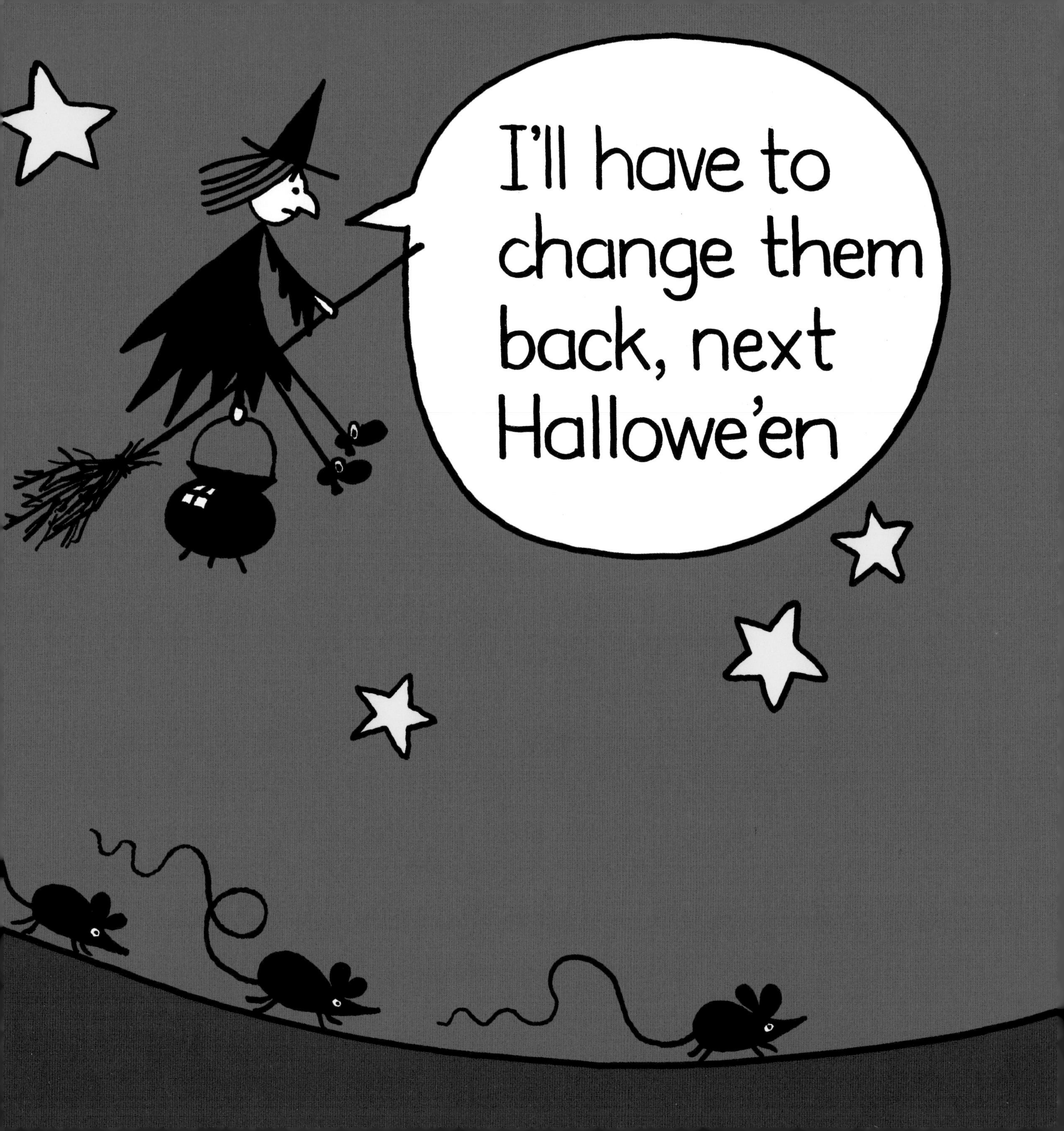
I'll have to change them back, next Hallowe'en

Goodbye!